LONGMAN ORIGINALS Stage Three
Series editor: Robert O'Neill

Dangerous Game

William Harris

Edited by L G Alexander

Illustrations by Biz Hull

Longman

Longman Group UK Limited,
Longman House, Burnt Mill, Harlow,
Essex CM20 2JE, England
and Associated Companies throughout the world

© Longman Group UK Limited 1977

First published 1977 in Longman Structural Readers
This edition first published 1992 in Longman Originals

Set in 11.5/13.5pt Melior, Adobe Linotype (postscript)

Produced by Longman Group (FE) Ltd
Printed in Hong Kong

ISBN 0 582 07495 9

Acknowledgements
The Publishers would like to thank Dr Jonathan Mestel
for acting as chess consultant.

Contents

CHAPTER ONE
Let me begin at the beginning

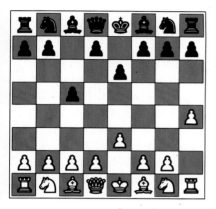

I don't know when the game began. My wife died twelve years ago and the game certainly began soon after that. But I can't remember when. I continued to live in this house after she died. I still live here. It's a big house and I live alone. I could move to a smaller place, but I don't want to leave. I love this house and every object in it. You see, I haven't got many friends, and all the objects in this house are important to me. I couldn't live without them.

Some time after my wife died, I realized that my bedroom was haunted. It's the only room in the house that's haunted. One night, I suddenly realized there was a ghost in the room. I wasn't afraid because this ghost was friendly. It was a happy ghost. I always wanted to laugh when it was in the room. You will say it was my wife's ghost. I don't know. I always think of the ghost as 'he', not 'she'. I named the ghost 'Poldy'. I invented the name 'Poldy' from the word 'poltergeist'. You know that a poltergeist is a playful ghost. It likes to drop things on the floor; it likes to make a noise; it likes to throw objects round the room. It likes to move your bed and to play games. Poldy was friendly and playful, so we invented a little game. We play it every night. We've been playing it for years now. In fact, I must *always* play the game before I go to sleep. I can't go to sleep if I don't play it. Poldy doesn't 'appear' at midnight or anything like that. He's not that kind of ghost. He's always in the room and he only appears when we play the game. Of course, I don't *have* to play the game, but, you see, I always *want* to play. I know Poldy does too. I'm writing this story because I want to tell you about this game. No one knows about it. My best friend (perhaps he's my only friend) doesn't know about it. *I* know about it and Poldy knows about it and that's all. It's our secret. But I'm talking too much. When you live alone, you're always talking to yourself! I must begin at the beginning.

My name is William Harris. I'm forty-eight years old. Perhaps you've heard of me. I'm not famous, but many people have heard of me. You see, I'm a writer. I've written about twenty-five books. I write all kinds of stories: love stories, detective stories and – yes, ghost stories. But don't get the wrong idea. This isn't just another ghost story. This is different from any story I've ever written. Why? Because it's a *true* story. All the events in this story have really happened. All the events in this story are true. In fact, they're still happening.

I'm not a famous writer, but my books sell quite well. I can afford to live in this nice house. I can afford to live in the way I want to live. I'm not rich, but I'm not poor. I live simply. I have always lived simply. When my wife was alive, I didn't live very simply. We went out a lot. We had a lot of friends. Since she died, I don't go out very much. I like to stay at home and write my books. (At the moment, I'm writing another detective story. My readers like my detective stories best. I invented the famous detective Filbert Wiley. Perhaps you have heard of him. Perhaps you have read one of my Filbert Wiley stories.) I've stopped work on my new Filbert Wiley to write this story. I have to write it now while there's still time.

But I must tell you something about myself first, and about my wife. Ah! Life was very different for me when she was alive. My wife's name was Julie. She was two years younger than I was. She was completely different from me. She liked to dance and sing; she liked to go to parties. Our house was always full of people in those days. "Put a suit on, William!" (I don't like suits) she used to say. "Put a suit on" meant many things. Perhaps we were going out. Perhaps friends were coming to dinner. Perhaps we were having a party. I never knew with Julie. Anything could happen. I never knew about it before it happened. My life was in Julie's hands. Without her I was nothing. I didn't want to meet the world, so Julie brought the world to me.

It was a wonderful life! It was wonderful because Julie made it like that. All our friends were jealous of me. "Lucky old William!" they used to say. "Lucky fellow to have a wife like that! He's so quiet and so uninteresting, and she's so *alive!*" Oh yes, they were jealous. You don't often see happy people, *really* happy people, I mean. And we were happy. That was our secret. Love was our secret. I loved Julie and she loved me. Then, suddenly, Julie fell ill, very ill. I called the best doctors, but they couldn't do anything. I looked after her day and night. But in two short months she was dead. Dead! I couldn't believe it. I still can't believe it after all these years. When she died, part of me died with her. Now she lives in my memory. I can't forget her and will never forget her. I didn't want to look for another wife. Julie had been my wife for twelve years and now she has been dead for twelve years. Sadly, we never had any children. So when she died, I was alone. I shut myself up in my house. I threw myself into my work. At first I wrote my books because I didn't want to think of my dear wife: the pain was too great. In time things were a little better, but the pain has never really gone. I still feel it sharply when I think of Julie. She is still alive in my memory.

Of course, I lost nearly all my friends – all those jealous friends. They liked Julie, but they didn't like me very much. Without Julie, I didn't go out. I didn't go to parties. I didn't ask other people to come to my house and all my 'friends' soon left me. No one was jealous of me any more. I wasn't 'lucky old William' any more; just 'poor old William'. Now I have only one real friend. His name is Louis. He's a writer too. But I don't know anything about his books. I haven't read any of them. In fact, I haven't seen his books in any bookshop. Louis and I never talk about books. That's because we have a common interest. We both like chess. We have a game of chess once a week. Louis comes to see me every Wednesday. He always arrives at eight o'clock in the evening and we play chess for about three hours. Sometimes we play a number of games; sometimes only one. At about eleven, Louis goes home and I go to bed and play a different kind of game with Poldy, but I'll tell you about that later. Louis is really a very good friend. We play chess and never talk very much. Sometimes we don't say anything all the evening. Good friends don't need to talk. You see, Louis knows me very well and I know him very well. We've been friends since we were students together. Louis was my friend before I met Julie. He knows a lot about me, but there are some things he doesn't know. I know he'll be surprised when he reads this story.

Louis and I have been playing chess together for years. He used to come here when Julie was alive. Julie and I never went to parties on a Wednesday, because that was always *my* day. I must tell you that Louis will be here tomorrow. It's Tuesday today. Tuesday morning. I'm sitting at my desk in my study. I'm writing this story. The winter sun is shining through my study window. It's a beautiful day, but I don't want to go out. I never want to go out these days. Filbert Wiley is my only company. At the moment I'm very tired: very, very sleepy because I didn't sleep well last night. I played a game with Poldy and it went on and on and on. I'll tell you about this game, but not just yet.

Well, that's my life. It's a very simple life and not a very interesting one, is it? How can life without Julie be interesting any more? Here I am, a middle-aged writer, alone in a big house. I have only one real friend in the world. I have my books. I have Filbert Wiley, the famous detective. Perhaps I live through Filbert. I have my chess and I have my memories. But it's not a sad life and it's not a very quiet life. A lot happens in this house. There's a lot of noise and laughter and… that's because I have Poldy. And I haven't told you anything about Poldy – yet! Poldy and laughter go together – I mean they used to go together!

I don't know when the game began. I've already told you that. I can't remember when I first met Poldy. But I can remember very clearly *how* I met him. I can remember the first moment he 'appeared': that is, when I realized he was in my bedroom. I can remember every detail. So I want to tell you about it in detail. But first I must tell you that my bedroom wasn't haunted when Julie was alive. Or perhaps it was and I didn't realize it. I'll never know.

Do you believe in ghosts? I've written a number of ghost stories, but they were only stories. I never used to believe in ghosts. And I'm not certain now. But I know one thing: there is certainly a poltergeist in my bedroom. I can't say more than that.

Here are a few details about my bedroom. You need to know them before I can tell my story. There's a big double bed in the room. Yes, it's the same double bed Julie and I slept in. The head of the bed is against a wall. I sleep on one side of the bed – the same side I have always slept on. There's a bedside table next to the bed. There's a bedside lamp on the table. There's a light socket near the floor. The light socket is for my lamp. My lamp has a long cord. There's a plug at the end of the cord and this plug goes into the light socket. Don't laugh at these details. They're all very important. You'll understand the reason soon enough.

One dark winter night I was reading in bed. It wasn't an interesting book and I was very sleepy. I usually switch off the lamp when I want to go to sleep. (My lamp has a small white switch.) But that night (I don't know why) I didn't switch off the lamp in the usual way. Instead, I leaned over the side of the bed and pulled the plug out of the socket. Why did I do this? I still don't know. It was a funny thing to do. The moment I pulled the plug out, I wasn't sleepy any more. Suddenly I was awake – really awake. The room was dark, completely black, but my eyes were wide open. My book fell to the floor. It hit the floor with a loud sound, but I didn't notice. I sat up in bed with my eyes open. I rested my back against the head of the bed. I looked into the dark room. Of course, I couldn't see anything. But at that moment, I knew there was someone in the room. I didn't know *where* in the room, but it? he? she? was somewhere in front of me. Many minutes passed. I looked hard into the dark. I waited, but I still couldn't see anything. I wasn't afraid. The 'person' in the room was very friendly. I was happy. I couldn't hear anything, but there was laughter in the air. "Who is it?" I called. "Who's there?" But there was no answer. I waited for a long time. The 'person' in the room was a friend, a good friend. I wanted to meet this friend very much. If I switch on the light, perhaps I'll see him, I thought. I pressed the switch on my bedside lamp. I pressed it on and off, but nothing happened. Then I remembered. I hadn't used the switch! I had pulled the plug out of its socket. So I leaned over the side of the bed and pushed the plug back into the socket. Suddenly the light came on. The room was empty. I could feel it. I knew the 'person' had gone. I pulled the plug out again and waited. Nothing. The room was still empty. I put the plug in and the light came on again. There was still no one there. I switched the light off (from the light switch), but nothing happened. I was alone. My friend had left me. I stayed awake for many hours. I thought: it's a poltergeist and at once the name 'Poldy' came into my head. I called out, "Poldy! Poldy!" but he didn't come back. In the end I fell asleep. But I knew something important had happened to me. This was my first meeting with the friendly ghost, my first meeting with Poldy. This was the beginning.

CHAPTER TWO
The game

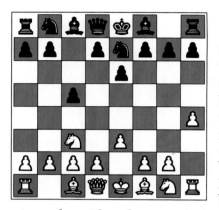

I woke up late the next morning. The cold winter sun was already up. My room was light. I sat up in bed and thought about the events of the night before. Had these things really happened? Was it all a dream? I looked over the side of the bed. Yes, my book was on the floor. I had dropped it there the night before. I looked at the lamp and the plug. The plug was in its socket. Yes, I had put it there the night before. The details were right. I got up slowly. I washed and had breakfast. Then I went to my study. (I was writing a detective story at the time, I remember.) The adventures of Filbert Wiley soon filled my day and I forgot about the adventures of the night before.

I finished work early. I wasn't sleepy in the evening, but I went to bed earlier than usual – at about ten o'clock. I sat in bed and thought about the night before. I didn't want to read, so I sat quietly with the light on. Then, very carefully, I switched it off (from the light switch) and waited. I looked into the dark room. Nothing happened. The room was 'empty'. This is silly, I thought. I switched the light on again and got a book – an interesting one this time. I read for a long time and began to get sleepy. I put my book on the bedside table. Then I wanted to switch the light off. But I didn't use the switch – I don't know why. Instead, I leaned over the side of the bed and found the cord. Then I found the plug and pulled it out of the socket. The moment I did this, I knew Poldy was there. The friendly ghost was somewhere in the room. "Poldy!" I called. There was no answer. I looked into the dark. I got out of bed and walked round the room. Poldy was there. I knew it. In the end, I went back to bed. I leaned over the side and pushed the plug into its socket. The light came on. Poldy had gone. When I switched the light off again (from the switch) he didn't come back. I switched the light on and off a number of times, but nothing happened. So I went to sleep.

The next night I made an important discovery. It was my first important discovery: the first of a number of discoveries. I went to bed at my usual time. I didn't read. Instead, I switched off the light (from the light switch) and waited for Poldy, but he didn't 'appear'. But the moment I pulled the plug out of the socket, he 'appeared'. That is, I felt he was there. When I put the plug back in, he 'disappeared'. This was my important discovery: Poldy *never* 'appeared' when I used the light switch. He appeared *only* when I pulled the plug out. He only appeared *once*. When I put the plug back in, he disappeared and he didn't come back.

I tried this the night after. I pulled the plug out the moment I went to bed. Poldy was there. I put it back and the light came on: Poldy had gone. I pulled the plug out again, but he didn't come back. After that I put it back and pulled it out a number of times, but nothing happened. So I knew. Poldy came only *once*: the moment I pulled the plug out. He went away the moment I put it back.

For many nights after that, I enjoyed Poldy's company. Sometimes I sat in the dark for hours with Poldy in the room. I enjoyed my power. I would 'bring' him into the room or I could 'send him away' with the light plug, but I could only do it once. I could keep the plug out of its socket for a long time. In that way I was able to enjoy Poldy's company for hours and hours. I was *happy* when Poldy was in the room. I often called to him, but he never gave me any sign of his presence. I could only 'feel' his presence: there was no other sign.

I never told anyone about Poldy. Louis came on Wednesdays and we played chess, but I never told him my secret. One Wednesday evening he said to me: "You're very well, William. Always smiling and happy. It's nice to see you like this. Perhaps you have a secret life!" I smiled and said nothing. It was true of course: I had a secret life, but I didn't tell Louis about it. I know he's my best, my only friend, but I don't think he can understand things like this.

I enjoyed Poldy's company in this way for nearly a year. Then one night something strange happened. I had pulled the plug out and Poldy was in my room. I was sitting in bed. I called out to him: "Poldy!" and he gave me the first sign of his presence. I heard a knock. It came from the other side of the room. Then there was another knock. The knocks got louder and came nearer and nearer to my bed. Then the knock stopped. I wasn't afraid: in fact, I laughed. Then the knock began again: it moved away from my bed to the other side of the room. It was a strange knock. How can I describe it? Well, it was like someone with a wooden leg. It was like a wooden leg on the floor. It was like someone with a limp. When a man walks with a limp, you can hear a knock. Knock, knock, knock – like that. I was very happy. At last I had a sign from Poldy. I could feel he was there and hear he was there. He can trust me, I thought. So he's given me a sign.

Every day I worked in my usual way, but my life was different now. Every night I enjoyed Poldy's company. He trusted me more and more. He gave me different signs of his presence. Sometimes he shook my bed. I laughed and he shook it again. Or sometimes he shook a chair in my room. I could hear it on the floor. Or sometimes he threw objects round the room. I couldn't see them in the dark, but I could hear them. Once a hair-brush flew right past my face. Sometimes Poldy opened and shut my bedroom door. He did this very quickly a number of times. Sometimes he played little tricks. Once I found my shirt in my bed. Another time I found my shoe in my bed. I always laughed at these tricks. I think Poldy liked to hear laughter. When I laughed, he knocked at the window or shook my bed.

I tried hard to see him. I looked into the dark room, but I never saw anything. But I could feel his presence and I could certainly hear him.

When I got tired of all these tricks, I pushed the plug back into its socket. The light came on and Poldy went away. Then I always switched it off and went to sleep.

One night, I made my second important discovery. Poldy was in my room. He 'limped' to my bed and away from it many times. He shook my bed and knocked at my door. In the end, I was very sleepy. I'll put the plug back in, I thought. The light will come on and Poldy will go away. Then I'll turn it off and go to sleep. I leaned over the side of the bed and picked up the plug. Suddenly, Poldy pulled the cord and the plug flew out of my hand. I had to find it (and it wasn't easy) and I put it in the socket. But I made an important discovery. Poldy didn't just want to give me signs of his presence. He didn't just want to play little tricks. He wanted to play a game with me.

In the end, we invented this game with the light plug. The rules of the game were very simple, but it took us a long time to invent them. I could say the rules 'grew'. They were like this:

Rule 1: I went to bed with the light still on.

Rule 2: I pulled out the plug from the socket and Poldy appeared. I didn't only feel his presence: he always gave me a clear sign. I heard 'knock, knock' at the other side of the room.

Rule 3: Poldy then began to 'limp' towards my bed. I had to put the plug back in the socket *before* he reached my bed. Poldy had to reach my bed *before* I put the plug back in. That was the game. If Poldy reached my bed before I put the plug in, he 'won'. He shook my bed and the game began again. If I put the plug in first, I won. Poldy disappeared when the light came on and didn't return.

We played this game every night for a long time, perhaps two years. Poldy usually won a number of times each night. I laughed a lot when we played. It was a very happy game. And then something went wrong. I don't know what and I don't know how. But something went wrong, very wrong.

CHAPTER THREE
A game of chess

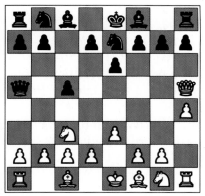

"Your move," Louis said.

"My move?" I answered. "I've just moved."

"No," Louis said. *"I've* just moved. It's your move." He pointed at the chess board.

"Don't be silly, Louis!" I said sharply. "I know when I've moved and when I haven't moved."

"Well, you haven't moved and it's your move," Louis repeated. "You haven't been watching the game, William."

"The game?" I cried suddenly. "Which game? Who told you about the game? What do you know about the game? I've never told anyone about the game. It's my secret. Do you understand? It's my secret. Just Poldy and I... We..." I was shouting. I could hear my voice. I stopped suddenly. Louis was looking at me strangely.

"Is there anything you want to tell me, William?"

"Eh? What?"

"Is there anything you want to tell me? There's something on your mind."

"There isn't anything on my mind," I said. I must pull myself together, I thought. I looked up at Louis. "You're right," I said. "There *is* something on my mind. It's this new Filbert Wiley story. It's on my mind all the time. It's a story about a game. The game is on my mind. I'm sorry I spoke like that a moment ago."

"That's quite all right," Louis said kindly. "Your story must be very interesting, but at this moment we're playing a game of chess."

"Yes, I must pull myself together," I said.

"Who is this... this Poldy?" Louis asked.

"Poldy?" I cried. "What do you know about Poldy? Who told you about Poldy?" I could hear my angry voice again. I was shouting. Again, I stopped suddenly. "I'm sorry," I said.

"You told me about Poldy, William," Louis said. "A moment ago you said: 'Just Poldy and I... We...'"

"Did I say that?" I asked.

"Yes," Louis said. "I know you very well, William. You haven't got many friends. Is this Poldy a new friend? Poldy is a very unusual name, isn't it?"

"It is an unusual name," I said. "I'll tell you about Poldy if you want to hear about him. Poldy is only a character in my new Filbert Wiley story."

"What sort of character?"

"I don't know. He's a playful character. He plays all kinds of tricks."

"I mean, is he a 'goody' or a 'baddie'?" Louis asked.

"Oh, he's a 'goody'," I said at once. "A very... very nice – er – person. He's kind and funny and I like him a lot, but... but..."

"Yes?"

"Well, sometimes I think he's a 'baddie' too. Poldy's character isn't clear in my mind. Sometimes I think he's evil. You know, *very* evil."

"Evil? But you said he's funny and kind and playful."

"That's an interesting point," I said. "Tell me, Louis. Can a person be evil and funny and kind and playful at the same time? What do you think?"

"I've never thought about it," Louis said.

"Let me tell you about Poldy, if I can," I said. "Let me try to tell you. Poldy..."

Suddenly I heard a loud 'knock, knock' from upstairs. Louis and I were in the living room. The living room is below my bedroom. The 'knock, knock' had come from my bedroom.

"What's the matter, William?" Louis asked. "Your face is

white. You were telling me about Poldy. Please go on."

"Did you hear a knock, Louis?" I asked. "Like this." I picked up a wooden chess piece and knocked on the table "Like a wooden leg on the floor. Like a man with a limp."

"No, of course not," Louis said. "I didn't hear anything."

"But it came from upstairs."

"No. It's very quiet in here."

"Then it must be my imagination."

"Yes," Louis answered. "It's your imagination. You *are* a writer, William, and you live in your imagination. But you must be careful. Imagination can be dangerous."

"In what way dangerous?"

"Well, it can control your life. You're working too hard. You don't go out enough. You lead an uninteresting life – in the real world, I mean. You're in your study all day. You're alone in this big house. Then at night you sleep and the next day you're in your study again. You need friends. You need the air and the sky and the sun. You don't live as a *person* but only through your imagination. And that's dangerous because adventures in the mind can control your life. You talk about this Poldy and you think he's a real person. But he's only a character in one of your stories. He's just like Filbert Wiley. He isn't real. He doesn't exist."

"Oh, but he *does* exist."

"Yes, but only in your mind."

"So he exists and is real. Hamlet was one of Shakespeare's characters. But he *exists.* He's real. Queen Elizabeth I existed. She was alive and she ruled England, but she's not *more real* than Hamlet. Don't you think that Hamlet is a real person – like Queen Elizabeth was a real person? I mean they are both real persons in our minds."

"That's an interesting philosophical point," Louis said. "Things can exist in the mind or in the real world. So the character in your story – this Poldy – is 'real' to you. And I am 'real' to you in the same way. Right?"

"Right," I said.

"I always knew you were a philosopher, William," Louis said. "Now let's get back to this game of chess. It's your move."

"My move? I've just moved."

"Let's not start that again. Look, we'll go through the moves from the beginning. I'm white and you're black. Right?"

"Right."

Louis went through the game from the beginning.

"We've both moved fourteen times," Louis said. "I'm white so I moved first. Now I've just moved again: that's the fifteenth move. And it's your move."

I looked at the chess board hard for a long time. "You're right," I said. "I wasn't watching the game."

"Yes, I told you that," Louis answered. "Your mind is on other things."

"Well, I'm looking at the game now and I don't like it. It has gone wrong."

"Not for me, but for you," Louis said.

"Yes," I answered. "Something's wrong, very wrong. I can't do anything about it." I moved my king.

Louis at once moved his queen. He picked up the big wooden chess piece and put it down hard on the chess board. It hit the board with a loud knock. "Check mate!" Louis said loudly. "I'm afraid you've lost the game."

I looked at the chess board. "You're right," I said. "The king is dead. I can't move him anywhere. It's check mate."

"You didn't play very well," Louis said. "You didn't play your usual game."

"I know," I answered.

"Do you know why?" Louis asked.

"No. Why? Tell me."

"Because your mind wasn't on the game. Your mind was on this character, Poldy. I didn't beat you. Poldy beat you."

"How?"

"Because he controls your mind. Philosophers and writers must *live* as well. They mustn't let ideas control their lives."

"You're right, Louis," I said.

Louis looked at his watch. "Mm," he said. "It's ten to twelve. It's late. I must go." He got up. "Thanks for the game, William. Good night and I'll see you next week."

"Thank you, Louis," I said. "Good night." I got up and suddenly knocked the chess board off the table. It hit the floor and the pieces went across the room.

"You've really lost the game now," Louis laughed.

CHAPTER FOUR
The game goes wrong

The game of chess I have just described was about five years ago. Of course, I have been playing chess with Louis once a week since then. I will have a game with him tomorrow. But I described this game of chess because I remember it in detail. At this time my game with Poldy was beginning to go wrong. This didn't happen suddenly. Oh, no. It was gradual, very gradual. I didn't really notice it at first.

Louis never spoke to me about Poldy again and of course *I* never spoke about Poldy. I had told Louis that Poldy was a character in my detective story and he believed me. I couldn't tell Louis that Poldy *really* exists. He doesn't exist only in my mind or in my imagination, but he exists in the real world. He lives in my room. Sometimes I don't think of it as my room any more, but as Poldy's room.

I nearly lost control of myself that night with Louis. I talked about Poldy and that was wrong. I know that Poldy heard me. The loud 'knock, knock' from upstairs was a warning. Of course Louis didn't hear it because it was a warning for me. Poldy was saying, "Be quiet, William! This is our secret, remember?" So I have been very careful since then. I never speak about my work because I don't want Louis to ask any questions about Poldy.

I said things began to go wrong and this happened gradually. I first noticed it about two months before the game of chess with Louis. One night, Poldy and I were playing our usual game. I had pulled the plug out of its

socket and the room was dark. I always 'feel' that Poldy is
there. After that he gives me a clear sign of his presence.
Sometimes he knocks on the floor, sometimes on the
window. Sometimes he shakes my bed. But this night Poldy
didn't give me a sign. I felt he was there when the light went
out. That was all. I sat up in bed and called to him. "Poldy!
You're there, I know. I'm ready to play. Are you ready?"

But nothing happened.

I got out of bed and walked round the room. I walked very
quietly across the wooden floor. My footsteps were very
light but I could hear them. While I was walking round the
room, I thought Poldy was behind me. I stopped suddenly
and turned round. Of course, I didn't see anything. I walked
up and down the room and stopped suddenly a number of
times. Poldy was following me. I stood still and listened.
Then I heard a soft knock on the floor. It was right behind
me. It got louder and louder. I turned round and it stopped.

I was angry. "What are you doing, Poldy?" I asked.
"You're not playing the game. Are you going to play the
game or aren't you? Very well," I said. "I'm going to punish
you. I'm going back to bed. I'm going to put the plug in and
send you away. I'm going to punish you."

I climbed back into bed. "I'll give you one more chance," I
said. "Do you want to play or not?" Again nothing
happened. "I'll count up to three," I said. I counted slowly.
"One. Two. Three." I leaned over the side of the bed and
touched the floor with my hand. I found the cord, but
suddenly the cord began to move through my hand. I held it
and pulled, but Poldy pulled too. I pulled with one hand
and I tried to find the plug with the other. I was nearly on
the floor now. I found the plug and pushed it in. The light
came on and Poldy had gone.

I switched off the light from the switch but lay awake for
a long time. My heart was beating wildly. That's funny, I
thought. Why doesn't he play? He's like a little boy. Perhaps
he wants to change the rules. He's playing tricks. But in my
heart I knew Poldy wasn't playing tricks. I had made my
third important discovery. Something had gone wrong with

our game. It would never be the same.

The night after that, I was afraid. I had never felt fear before in my games with Poldy, but this time I felt fear. I couldn't pull the plug out. I lay in bed a long time with the light on. I was really afraid. At last I was ready. What is going to happen? I thought when I pulled the plug out.

Poldy didn't play any tricks, I'm glad to say. We played our usual happy game. I enjoyed it and Poldy enjoyed it.

For many nights after that we played our game. Well, perhaps I've made a mistake, I thought. Nothing has changed. Poldy was only playing tricks that night. But I was wrong.

The night before my game of chess with Louis (the one I have already described) was very bad. There was a full moon that night, so I didn't draw the curtains. I had never done this before. The room was full of light. My light was on when I got into bed. After a short time, I pulled the plug out. I was ready to begin the game, but nothing happened. Poldy gave no sign. He was there, of course. I sat in bed and waited. I could see the full moon through my window. There were dark shadows on the floor. There were shadows on the walls. I could hear a cat outside. It was crying like a baby. I don't like that noise. I got up and opened the window. "Ssssh!" I cried. The cat stopped. Then it started again. "Ssssh!" I cried again. I saw the cat: a fat black one. It ran across the garden. Good, I thought. I went back to bed. "Are we going to play or aren't we?" I asked. I could see the whole room clearly. I could see the chair with my clothes on it. I could see the big wardrobe in the corner of the room. I looked at the wardrobe in the corner of the room. I looked at the wardrobe for a long time. Suddenly, the wardrobe door began to open very quietly. Just a little at first. Then more and more. Soon it was wide open.

I keep my clothes in the wardrobe. I haven't got many clothes because I don't need them. There are a few shirts, two pairs of trousers, two suits and an old coat.

The wardrobe door was wide open, so I could see inside. I saw my shirts, my suits and the coat. Then my coat began to move. It 'stepped' outside the wardrobe. It stood in front of the wardrobe door. "Poldy," I said slowly.

Poldy (or the coat) didn't listen to me. It stood there like a person: a person without a head or legs or hands. Then it began to 'walk' towards me. After a few slow steps, it raised an 'arm' and shook it at me.

I was angry with Poldy. "I've had enough of your silly tricks!" I cried. "I'm going to punish you. I'm going to send you away. If you won't play, then I must punish you." I leaned over the side of the bed and picked up the plug. It was easy to find in the moonlight. "See?" I asked and held up the plug. "I'm going to put it in the socket now and you're going to go away."

The coat moved suddenly towards me. An arm reached for the plug and took it from my hands. The cord went through my fingers and the lamp fell onto the floor.

I got up angrily. The coat dropped the plug and went back into the wardrobe quickly. The wardrobe door shut with a loud noise. I picked up the lamp and put it back onto the bedside table. Then I went towards the wardrobe. I opened it a little. I put my hand inside and felt the clothes. My coat was in its place. I could feel it. It was soft and empty. I pulled the wardrobe door open and looked inside. It was empty, quite empty: there was no sign of Poldy.

"I see," I said. "You want me to draw the curtains before we play." I went to the window and looked out. The black cat was there again. It was still crying like a baby. "Sh!" I shouted, but it didn't stop. I was getting ready to draw the curtain when I noticed something. Someone was standing behind the curtain. I could clearly see the shape of a figure behind the curtain. I tried to draw the curtain, but I couldn't. The figure wouldn't let me. "Oh!" I shouted angrily. "I've had enough!" I went back to bed and the curtain moved across the window. Now the room was in complete darkness. "So you want to play now," I said. There was no answer, of course – just the sound of the cat outside the window. I reached for the plug on the floor, found it and put it in the socket. The light came on. Poldy had gone.

Again I lay awake a long time. We had played a bad game, a very bad game. While I lay there, I could hear my heart. It was beating wildly. And I could hear the cat outside. It never stopped. It cried like a baby all night long.

CHAPTER FIVE
Good games and bad games

In the past five years, up to the present time, I've continued to play games with Poldy. We've played every night. We've played good games and bad games. I've already described the good games. They're very simple and always fun. I'm happy when I'm playing good games and sad when I'm playing bad ones.

In what way is a 'good' game different from a 'bad' game, you will ask. Well, I've already described a few bad games. Perhaps you've noticed that in a bad game there are no rules. Anything can happen. And another thing: when I'm playing a good game, I'm never afraid. But when I'm playing a bad game, my heart is full of fear. The bad games are like an evil warning.

I want to describe some of the games in the past five years. At the beginning (at the time of the game of chess I have already described) we didn't play many bad games. But after a time we played a good game one night and a bad game the next night. This was true up to two years ago. And this is when I began to worry. Worry and fear were always present in my life.

Why did Poldy begin to play bad games? I've often asked myself this question and I've never been able to explain why. I've thought of many different reasons. Perhaps you can think of a few reasons yourself. But it isn't easy to think of one thing and say this is the reason.

At first I thought Poldy was jealous. That is, perhaps he

was jealous when I won a game. So I let him win all the time. But he still wanted to play bad games.

Perhaps Poldy wanted to punish me. What had I done? I thought about this a lot. Perhaps Poldy was angry because I told Louis about him. But I didn't tell Louis anything. I said Poldy was a character in one of my detective stories. I didn't say he was a ghost, a poltergeist. And don't forget the bad games had begun *before* I said anything to Louis.

Who *is* Poldy? I've often thought about this, too. If I learn the answer to this question, perhaps I'll have the answer to my first question: Why does he want to play bad games? But I can't find the answer. I've often asked myself: Is Poldy the ghost of my dead wife? Is 'Poldy' really 'Julie'? I think the answer to this question must be: No. Poldy has never given me any sign. For example, there's a photo of Julie on my bedroom wall. Poldy could shake it or move it, but he has never done that. I've kept one of Julie's dresses. It's a beautiful party dress. It's in my wardrobe. Poldy has never 'touched' it. He has often taken *my* clothes out of the wardrobe. If Poldy is Julie, he – or she – can easily give me a sign. Remember, Julie loved me and I loved her. So Poldy can't be Julie, but I'm not really certain.

Is Poldy just part of my imagination? No, a thousand times no. Why? Because all these things really happen. I don't imagine them. They are *facts*. Poldy *exists*.

Poldy and I gradually played more and more bad games. Then I began to worry. I only wanted to play good games. How could I avoid bad ones? I tried to avoid them in a number of ways. I'll describe some of these ways to you.

I always know when we're going to play a bad game. I can feel evil in the air before the game begins. This is one thing I've tried to do: I've tried to pull the plug out and put it back at once. In this way, Poldy doesn't have a chance to play. He goes away when the plug goes back in. Poldy was surprised when I first did this. It worked very well. But now he won't let me do it. He knows when I'm going to try.

Here's another way I've tried. Remember, Poldy only

haunts my bedroom. He never haunts another part of the house. I've tried to sleep in other rooms in my house. But I can't avoid a bad game like that. One night, I slept in my study. I had a strange dream. I dreamt that I was sleeping in my study. In my dream, I got up and went to my bedroom. I sat in my own bed and read a book with the light on. In my dream, I pulled the plug out – and then, suddenly, I woke up. I wasn't in my study when I woke up, but in my bedroom. I was leaning over the side of the bed. The plug was in my hand. I had walked in my sleep. Poldy did this: he drew me back to the bedroom through my dream.

I tried another thing. I tried *not* to play the game. One night, I sat in bed with the light on. Then I turned the light off from the switch. Of course (this is always the rule) Poldy didn't appear. I went to sleep easily. But during the night I suddenly woke up and switched on the light. I don't know why. I had to. Then I pulled the plug out and the game began. This happened a number of times.

You will ask me: Why don't you sell your house and go away? I've asked myself this question too. The fact is, I can't. I've often thought about it, but I can't do it. I've tried another thing. I've left my house at night and gone to a hotel. But when I do this, I can't sleep. I always leave the hotel during the night. I pay the bill at (say) four o'clock in the morning and go home. It isn't easy to leave a hotel at four in the morning! (Try it and see!) After that I go to bed and play a game with Poldy. So, you see, I can never avoid a game. Poldy always finds a way to draw me back to my bedroom.

Up to a year ago we had played very many bad games. But Poldy had never 'touched' me. I had tried to catch objects and to 'touch' him. But he had never 'touched' me. This was a kind of rule. I can't describe my panic and terror when Poldy first 'touched' me.

It all happened one night about a year ago. I went to bed at eleven o'clock. I knew it was going to be a 'bad' night and not a 'good' night. I could feel it. I read for hours because I didn't want to pull the plug out. In the end, I was very sleepy, but of course I couldn't sleep. I leaned over the side of the bed in my usual way and pulled the plug out. At once my eyes were wide open and I was awake. Poldy was there and we were ready for the game. During a bad game, Poldy doesn't always give a clear sign of his presence, but that night he gave a very clear sign at once. I lay in bed in terror and waited. Nothing happened for a moment and then the bed began to move. Poldy wasn't shaking the bed. He was raising it off the floor! The bed moved into the air. I leaned over the side and tried to touch the floor. I tried to find the plug. But I couldn't reach the floor. The bed was (I think) about three feet above the floor! Then the bed began to turn round: slowly at first. It went round and round and round, first slowly, then faster and faster and faster and faster! Suddenly, it stopped in the air and dropped to the floor quickly. It touched the floor lightly and was in its usual place: the head of the bed was against the wall with the bedside table beside me. I tried to reach the plug. I touched the floor with my fingers and found it. I tried to put it back and then Poldy slapped my hand sharply! I dropped the plug in terror. He had never touched me before, but now he had slapped me!

I lay back in bed. The room was quiet. The bed didn't move. Then I felt something above my head. It was like a bird. I put my hand above my head. There was nothing there. Then something touched my hair lightly – like a soft hand. Fingers went lightly through my hair!

I jumped out of bed and ran to the other side of the room. I heard footsteps behind me. I turned round. Poldy was behind me. I turned round again and again, but Poldy was always behind me. Then he slapped me in the face!

Then he began to pinch me. He gave me a little pinch at first: a little pinch on the face, a soft pinch. After that he began to pinch my arms and legs very hard. I kicked and shouted, but I couldn't stop him. I jumped back into bed and – you will never believe it – Poldy bit my face very hard! I cried out in pain. I leaned over the side of the bed and

touched the floor. I touched it wildly to find the plug. At last the plug was in my hand. I tried to find the socket. I touched the wall with my fingers, but in my panic I couldn't find it. "Please! Please!" I shouted. "Where is it? Where's the socket?" A great power tried to pull the plug out of my hand. But in my terror I was strong – stronger than Poldy. I pushed the plug in hard. The light came on – and suddenly, I was alone. "Ah!" I cried, while my heart beat wildly and my body shook in panic and terror.

That was a very bad night. It was the first time Poldy had touched me. After that he often touched me. Sometimes he touched softly with his fingers, sometimes he pinched, slapped or kicked. It wasn't just a bad game any more. It was a dangerous game.

I've already told you, we began to play more and more bad games. But the number of bad games and good games was the same. That was true a year ago. But after Poldy touched me the first time something changed. We never played another good game. During the past year we have played only bad games every night. All our games are bad, but they're not all the same. Some are just 'bad'; others are very, very bad and very dangerous. Poldy has become completely evil. He only shows me the evil side of his character. My bedroom is an evil place. It's evil in the day-time. It's evil when Poldy isn't there. It's evil all the time. What can I do? I don't know. I just don't know.

Up to a month ago, I was all right during the day. I went to my study every day and wrote. This took my mind off Poldy. I thought of new adventures for Filbert Wiley and this gave me pleasure. But during the past month I haven't been able to work. I still come to my study every day, but I sit at my desk and look out of the window. I don't write anything. I sleep very little. I eat very little. I am thin and weak. But today I'm writing. I'm writing these words. I'm writing quickly before it's too late. I have to write this story of my life with Poldy before it's too late.

You will ask: Why don't you tell Louis about this?

Louis still comes on Wednesdays and we still play chess. I never play chess well now and he always beats me. I'm always tired and worried.

"What's the matter with you, William?" Louis asked last week. "I can't understand. You're ill. You must see a doctor. I'm worried about you. If you don't call a doctor, I'll call one myself."

Of course I can't let Louis call a doctor. "Look," I said. "I know I'm not very well, but I'll be better soon. I'm writing a very strange story about Filbert Wiley. I'll be better when I finish the story. I know I will. So please don't call a doctor. Do you promise?"

"All right, William," Louis said. "I promise."

Louis is a good friend and I know he'll keep his promise.

Have I tried to tell Louis about Poldy? Yes, I have. Many times. But every time I try, I can't speak. I've tried to ask Louis to stay in the house with me for a whole night, but again, I can't. When I try to open my mouth, I can't. Then I always hear that 'knock, knock' from the room above. I always hear a warning from Poldy. The words 'It's our secret' come into my head. Perhaps a real voice speaks these words. Perhaps it's Poldy's voice. It speaks kindly, but there's always a warning in the voice.

One Wednesday about two months ago, I was playing chess with Louis. I was very tired. The night before had been very bad. I tried to play chess and I didn't think of Poldy, but Louis suddenly remembered the name 'Poldy' and spoke to me during the game.

"William," Louis said. "I was in a bookshop the other day and I was looking at your latest books – the Filbert Wiley stories. I remember once – perhaps it was five years ago – you spoke to me about a new character. You called this character 'Poldy'. I've never forgotten his name because it's a strange name. I don't *like* the name, but I've certainly remembered it. I bought all your latest books and took them home. I read them all and enjoyed them, but I didn't find this character 'Poldy' in any of them."

My face was white. Poldy was knocking hard on the floor of the room above. I could hear it, but Louis couldn't. In the end I said, "Yes, Louis. I didn't use this character in my story. I changed the story."

"Why?" Louis asked. "I remember he was an interesting character, both good and evil."

"No," I shouted. "He's evil, evil, only evil!" The knock on the floor above was louder and louder. It was like a wild dance. I heard the warning and pulled myself together. "I'm sorry," I said in a quiet voice. "No, I didn't use this character." (I couldn't say the name 'Poldy'.)

We continued to play chess. The game ended in the usual way. Louis said "Check mate" and I lost. My king was dead. Louis said goodnight and left.

That night Poldy really punished me. He pinched, kicked and slapped. The funny thing is: there are never any marks on my body. I'm often in great pain, but he never leaves any marks. Then I made my fourth important discovery: Poldy didn't like Louis. He didn't want him to come to my house. He wanted to be alone with me all the time. The games on Tuesday nights (the nights before Louis came) were always very, very bad.

I don't enjoy Tuesday evenings any more. I'm afraid of Tuesday nights. And it's Tuesday today!

CHAPTER SIX
Monday night

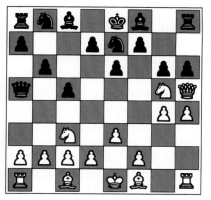

I want to tell you about last night in detail because we've never played a dangerous game like that before. I tremble when I think of it. I'm trembling at this moment while I'm writing these words.

But let me begin at the beginning. Yesterday I sat in my study all day long. Of course, I didn't write a word. I didn't try to write anything. Filbert Wiley doesn't interest me. His adventures mean nothing to me.

So how did I spend the day? I looked out of the window all day. It's winter now, but it isn't very cold. Yesterday the sky was clear. The sun shone in a blue sky. I looked down at my garden. It was quiet and empty. The grass was wet. The trees were without their leaves. Nothing happened all day. I only saw one sign of life: a fat black cat walked across the grass. It stood under my bedroom window and looked up at it for a long time. Then it went away very slowly. I remember that cat very well. I had seen it once before. I had heard it in my garden years ago – when my game with Poldy had begun to go wrong. The cat didn't worry me now. It wasn't important. My only worry was Poldy.

Perhaps you're thinking: there's no need to worry. I can go away for ever. I don't *have* to play games with a ghost. But I *want* to play. This game is part of my way of life. It is forever in my mind. So I must stay here to the end.

I know you want to hear about the events of last night. But you must give me time. I need time to get them in order.

Very many things happened and I want to remember them all.

The sky remained clear at night. There was a full moon. It was like a night I have already described in this story. I was glad there was a full moon. My room was full of light. I didn't draw my curtains before I went to bed. I had the moon for company. Perhaps it was midnight when I pulled the plug out and the game began at once.

Poldy surprised me at the beginning of the game. He didn't begin with a bad game but a good one. I couldn't believe it! We hadn't played a good game for a very long time. I was almost happy while we played. I didn't realize that this was a trick – an evil trick. At the beginning of the good game Poldy gave a clear sign of his presence. I heard a knock at the other side of the room. Then he began to limp towards my bed while I tried to find the plug. He reached my bed and shook it before I put the plug in. He had won. So we began again. I usually let him win during good games. But I didn't let him win last night. He really won. I always found the plug but Poldy was quicker than I was. This didn't worry me. But then something happened very suddenly and the good game stopped. I began to tremble. My room had become cold – very, very cold. I don't know why. My house is always warm. I hate the cold. It was at this moment that the good game stopped. I could suddenly feel evil in the air.

I wanted to be warm so I covered my head with the blankets and waited. A hand pulled the blankets off my bed very quickly. I sat up and watched. My blankets flew across the room and dropped onto the floor. I ran after them. But when I tried to reach them, they moved away from me. I think Poldy was saying, "Catch me if you can." I understood he wanted to play hide-and-seek with me. "Very well," I said loudly. "If you want to play hide-and-seek we'll play, but please give me my blankets." The blankets flew onto my bed. "Good," I said. "Now I'll count up to ten and you can hide." I turned my head towards the wall and began to count: "One, two, three…" I was counting very slowly.

While I was counting I heard footsteps behind me. I heard all kinds of little noises. Then the room was quiet. I turned round.

Of course the room was empty. Poldy had hidden. But where was he? You can't hide in many places in my room. You can hide under the bed, under the chair and in the wardrobe. But then Poldy is a ghost: he can hide anywhere. He can hide inside one of my pockets!

"I'm coming to find you, Poldy," I said.

I went straight to the wardrobe. I opened the door very slowly. Before the door was wide open, I put my hand inside the wardrobe carefully. Perhaps Poldy will bite or slap me, I thought. But he didn't. I pulled the door wide open. The moonlight shone into the wardrobe. I could see my clothes inside it. I could see my shirts, my trousers, my suits and my old coat. I could see Julie's beautiful dress. I touched all my clothes. Nothing. He's inside my coat, I thought. I took the coat out of the wardrobe and shook it. Nothing again. "Where are you?" I shouted. In a wild panic, I took my clothes out one by one and shook them. Then I threw them onto the bedroom floor. Soon all my clothes were on the floor. Julie's party dress was on the floor too.

The wardrobe was empty, but Poldy gave no sign.

"You're under the bed!" I cried. I lay on the floor and went under the bed. I touched the floor with my hands – but there was nothing. I got up and walked round the room. I looked under the chair. Nothing. In the end, I sat on the chair and waited. He was in the room. I could feel that, but I couldn't find him.

I sat on the chair for a long time. I was sleepy and shut my eyes. When I opened them I looked at my bed. This woke me up. Poldy had dropped the blankets onto the bed some time ago. The blankets were still there, but there was a shape under them. It was the shape of a person with blankets over his head. I went quietly towards the bed and touched the blankets. The 'figure' moved under them. It moved like a person in his sleep. I touched them again. The figure threw the blankets back. I couldn't see anyone, but I heard quick footsteps to the other side of the room. Poldy had been under the blankets.

"I've caught you!" I cried. "I've won! Now it's my turn to hide. You must count up to ten and I'll hide."

I waited and then I heard a knock from the corner of the room. He's counting, I thought. One knock, then another and another. Where can I hide? I thought. There was only one place: under the bed. I went under it very quietly and lay still. The knocks continued. There were ten of them, and then silence. I held my breath and listened. Complete silence. I looked across the floor. I could see the clothes I had thrown there. Then the clothes began to move. Someone was picking them up and throwing them again one by one. Shirts moved into the air and fell again. My trousers, my coat and my suits moved up and fell. Julie's dress shone in the moonlight: then it moved up and fell too. Poldy was going through all my clothes carefully.

Suddenly Poldy broke the silence. The wardrobe door flew open. He hit the wardrobe hard. The wardrobe shook. Then it fell and hit the floor with a loud noise. There was silence again. I held my breath. I heard the 'limp' from the other side of the room. It came towards the bed very slowly. Knock, knock, knock, nearer and nearer and nearer. I wanted to scream. Poldy stopped beside my bed. I was very cold now and I drew up my legs close to my body. Something touched my legs softly. I didn't move. Then something touched my face. I felt hot breath on my face and screamed loudly. I tried to move away but couldn't. In my fear I lay still. Then Poldy raised the whole bed above my head and dropped it on top of me. It hit the floor loudly but didn't touch me. Then he raised it again. It almost touched the ceiling above me. I looked up at it in terror and it began to come down very slowly. In a panic I stood up and ran to the other side of the room. I looked at the bed. It returned to the floor softly. I must hide somewhere, I thought. The wardrobe was on the floor in front of me. I turned it over. Then I climbed inside it and shut it. I lay there quietly.

Poldy began to knock at the wardrobe door, very quietly at first, then louder. Suddenly the door flew open. A strong pair of hands took hold of me, picked me up and threw me onto the bed. I screamed and shouted, but I didn't feel any pain. I got under the blankets and waited.

For the first time I heard Poldy's 'voice'. I heard a long evil laugh. There was something in the voice that I recognized. Soon the room was full of wild laughter.

"Stop it! Stop it! Please stop it!" I cried. The laughter continued for a long time and then stopped.

There was a very long silence after this. The game of hide-and-seek had ended. What's he going to do next? I thought. Perhaps half an hour passed and nothing happened.

Then I heard a strange noise. Someone was scratching. It was like fingers on glass. Was Poldy scratching the windows? I looked at them carefully and could see them clearly in the moonlight, but the sound didn't come from the windows. There isn't any more glass in the room, I thought. But I was wrong. There was the photo of Julie on the wall! The photo was behind glass. I listened. The scratching continued. The sound came from the picture. I looked at the picture carefully. It was a life-size photo of Julie's face. There she was, young and beautiful. She was smiling at me. In the moonlight, I couldn't see the details, of course. But I knew that photo so well! It was easy for me to imagine Julie's beautiful face. The scratching stopped and the photo moved off the wall and flew towards me slowly. Soon it was a few feet away from me. I looked into Julie's eyes and she looked into mine. "Is it you, Julie? Are you the ghost? Are you haunting me?" The answer to my questions was evil laughter. Julie had always laughed softly, but I recognized her laugh in this evil laughter.

The photo stopped five feet above the floor. Then something strange happened. Julie's dress moved off the floor. It moved up towards the photo. Soon it was under the photo. Then the dress began to dance. It danced very beautifully – just like Julie used to dance. Julie's 'head' was the photo. Her 'body' was the dress. Only Julie could dance like that. Then I knew for the first time: Julie and Poldy were the same 'person'. The dance was a clear sign. I had never wanted to believe that Poldy was Julie, but now I had to believe it.

CHAPTER SEVEN

The truth

I've told you the truth in this story, but I haven't told you the whole truth. Why? Because I haven't been able to admit the truth to myself, so how could I admit it to you? I've avoided the truth for twelve years now. But the time has come to admit it. Perhaps you already know. Yes, I killed Julie. But please don't mistake me. I killed her out of love not hate. I had to kill her for her own good.

I've told you that Julie loved me and I loved her. That's true. I've told you that Julie and I were happy. That's true too. I've told you that my friends were jealous of me. That's also true. But I haven't told you one thing: I was jealous of my friends.

You know a lot about me now. You know I'm not an interesting person. I don't go out much. I don't dance. I haven't got many friends. My life is in my books. In our twelve years together, Julie changed my life. She filled my life with friends and with laughter. So why did I kill her?

We used to go out together a lot. Friends used to come to our house a lot. Julie liked company. She liked my company, but she liked other people's company too. But I wanted Julie for myself and only for myself. At parties I was always alone. There were always young men round Julie. They were always dancing with her. She enjoyed their company. Of course, Julie was faithful to me and I was faithful to her. But that wasn't enough for me. I didn't want Julie to speak to other men. I didn't want her to dance with other men. I wanted her to be with *me* all the time. When I saw other men round her I was always jealous. I couldn't control my jealousy. One day I spoke to her about it. I can't remember our exact words, but they were something like this:

"Put your suit on, William. We're going out tonight."

"I don't want to go out," I answered.

"Don't be silly, William. We're going *out*."

"But I want to stay here," I said.

"You always want to stay at home," Julie said. "I know you want to write your books but we must live too."

"But I don't like to be with so many people," I said. "I only want to be with you."

"William!" Julie said kindly. "You're jealous."

I had to admit it. "I know I am," I said.

"There's no need to be jealous," she said. "I love you and you know it."

"Yes, I know it very well."

"Your character is different from mine. I *need* a lot of people round me," Julie said. "I can't be in this house all the time – alone with you."

"I'm afraid I'll lose you," I said.

"You must never fear that," Julie said. "You'll never lose me. I love you and I'm your wife."

"I want you to be my wife for ever," I said.

"And I will be," Julie answered.

She was telling the truth, but I was still very jealous. In time, I got more and more jealous. I couldn't control it any more.

Then something happened. I've already told you about it. Julie fell ill. She was very, very ill. I've told you I called the best doctors and that's true. "Your wife is very ill," one of them said to me. "She has a weak heart. She must be careful. She could die very suddenly."

I was afraid to lose Julie. I wanted her to live. But I wanted her to be mine for ever. Then an evil idea came into my mind. I thought: I can kill Julie and she will be mine. After that I'll never go out and she'll always be with me. I

thought about this idea a lot and I knew I had to kill her.
That's why I've never looked for another wife since Julie.
She is with me all the time: I have her pictures and I have
my memories of her. I'm not jealous any more because I
don't need to be jealous.

One night she lay beside me. She was very ill and was
breathing softly. She was awake and I spoke to her.

"Julie," I whispered. "I want you to be mine for ever. You
love me and I love you. That's the secret of our happiness."

"Yes, that's our secret," she whispered.

"You'll always stay with me in this house," I said.

"Yes," she whispered.

Then, very softly, I put my pillow over her face and held
it there. I held it there for a long time. She tried to move
away, but she couldn't. She was very weak. I could hear her
cries, but I didn't take the pillow away. At last her heart
stopped. She was dead.

"That's our secret," I said when she had died. "Now
you're mine for ever."

I phoned the doctor at once. I said that Julie wasn't
breathing very well. The doctor arrived quickly, but of
course, Julie was dead.

"I'm sorry to say this, Mr Harris," he said, "but your wife
is dead. Her heart has stopped. She died a short time ago.
Perhaps she died in her sleep."

I cried a lot, but in my heart I was glad. I was glad because
Julie was mine for ever.

Today it's Tuesday, January 22nd. I killed my darling
Julie twelve years ago today.

CHAPTER EIGHT
Monday night continued

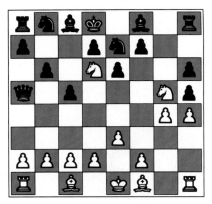

I broke off my story because I wanted to tell you the truth. You think I'm mad, I know, and perhaps I *am* mad. I've lived with this secret for twelve years now: I am a murderer. I murdered my wife. My house has been haunted since then. And last night I realized the truth for the first time in twelve years. The ghost in my bedroom isn't a playful poltergeist. Its name isn't 'Poldy'. It's the ghost of my dear wife, Julie. It was a playful ghost at first, but now it's jealous and evil – like I was twelve years ago.

Last night, I suddenly saw Julie 'alive' again. Her 'head' was the photo; her 'body' was the dress. She was dancing round the room. Oh, she danced very beautifully! Her beautiful dress was shining in the moonlight. I sat in bed and watched her. I forgot about the evil laughter. I forgot about my fears and worries. I forgot about our game. I could only think of Julie – 'alive' again after all these years. "It's not possible," I said to myself. "I can't believe it." Julie continued to dance and dance. I could hear music in my mind. I suddenly saw myself at a party. There was noise and laughter in the room. There were young men all round the room. My Julie was dancing to the music and the young men were looking at her. Then they looked at me and laughed. While they were laughing at me, I became angry and jealous. My mind became full of evil. "Go away!" I screamed at the young men. "Julie is mine, mine! Can't you see?" The young men laughed louder and louder. I became angrier and angrier. I jumped out of bed and ran towards the dancing ghost. The music continued to play in my mind. The young men continued to watch me and to laugh at me. I picked up a chair and hit the young men with it. Then I hit the dancing ghost. I hit the beautiful dress while it was moving round the room. Suddenly, the music in my mind stopped. The dancing stopped. The young men in the room disappeared. Their faces became shadows – then nothing. Their laughter stopped.

I hit the dress again, not the picture, but just the dress. It trembled and shook, then it fell slowly to the floor. The photo was still at the top of the dress. The photo and the dress lay on the floor. Julie's smiling eyes looked up at me from the floor. "They've gone," I whispered. "The young men have gone. You're mine again. All mine."

I stood beside the dress and looked at it for a long time. Nothing happened: it didn't move. I touched it. It was real. I touched the photo. It was real too. Julie's eyes smiled at me from behind the glass. "I want you to be mine for ever," I said to the photo and I went back to my bed and got a pillow. Then I returned to the dress on the floor. I put the pillow over the photo and held it there. I held it there for a long time. The dress tried to move away but couldn't. Soft cries came from the photo. In the end the dress didn't move any more. I smiled to myself. I've murdered Julie a second time, I thought. I laughed loudly.

Suddenly, a great scream came from the photo on the floor. One scream, then another and another. I jumped back in fear. The screaming stopped. The photo of Julie began to change. It wasn't smiling any more. It was crying. I touched the glass on the photo. It was wet. Then the photo moved away from my hand. I stood up. The photo began to move off the floor very, very slowly. It came towards me and stopped in front of my face. Then it fell to the floor and the glass broke into a thousand pieces. A 'hand' began to tear the photo into little pieces. It tore the hair, the eyes, the nose, the mouth. Soon there were little pieces of paper on the floor beside the dress. Then a great wind blew through the room. It blew the dress across the floor. It blew the little pieces of paper to every part of the room. They fell to the floor slowly like snow. Then the wind dropped.

The ghost was still in the room. I could feel it. That's the end of the game, I thought. I'll go back to bed and put the plug in. I've had enough of this. I picked up the pillow from the floor and went back to bed.

I was very tired and wanted to sleep. I leaned over the side of the bed to find the plug. I'll send the ghost away and go to sleep, I thought. I touched the plug, but the moment I touched it I heard evil laughter. Then I realized the game hadn't finished!

The plug moved away from my hand. I tried to find it again. Every time I touched it, it moved away. I took hold of the cord and 'followed' it with my fingers. Then I found the plug again but couldn't pick it up. It moved across the floor. I got out of bed. I was on my knees on the floor. I could see the plug in the moonlight. I could see it very clearly. I went towards it on my knees. When I reached it, it moved away again. The evil laughter continued. "Please, Julie," I said. "Please give me the plug." The plug came towards me and danced in front of my eyes, but I couldn't touch it. "I'm not going to play any more," I said. "I'm leaving the room." I got up and went towards the door.

I tried to open the door but couldn't. I banged the door hard with my hands. I pushed and pulled but I couldn't open it! I was a prisoner in my own room. "Where can I go? What can I do?" I cried. "I'm your prisoner now. Please let me go. Please! Please!"

The evil laughter stopped. The room was silent. Then something banged lightly against the window. After this I heard a scratching sound – like fingernails on glass. It isn't the glass over Julie's photo, I thought. I listened again. The sound was coming from the window. I went towards it and looked out. There was a face at the window – not Julie's face or the face of any person. It was the face of a cat! The cat had climbed up to my window and was outside. It was looking into my room. It wasn't the fat black cat I had seen in the morning. It was a white cat. I had seen this cat before somewhere, but where? I tried to think. Suddenly I remembered. Of course! It was Julie's cat. Julie loved animals. She had had a cat like this when she was alive: a beautiful white cat.

When Julie died – I mean, after I murdered her – the cat disappeared. I never saw it again. But now it had returned. I looked through the window. The cat's face was against mine. Only the glass was between us. The cat's eyes were red and angry. It scratched the glass wildly. I banged the glass from the inside, but the cat wouldn't go away. It began to cry like a baby. "Stop it! Stop it!" I screamed.

I ran back to the bedroom door and tried to open it. Again, it wasn't possible. The cat continued to cry outside the window. I suddenly wanted to kill it. I looked round the room and tried to find something. I was mad with anger. My wardrobe was still on the floor. Pieces had broken off it. I picked up a thick piece of wood and ran towards the window.

The cat looked at me with its red eyes. It cried louder and louder. I hit the window hard with the piece of wood. It broke into a thousand pieces. I laughed with pleasure. Then I looked through the broken window, but there was nothing there. No cat, no sound, nothing! Wonderful, I thought. It's gone away. Perhaps it was never there. Perhaps I only imagined it. I must pull myself together. I'm imagining things.

But I wasn't imagining things. I heard a sound behind me and jumped. It was the sound of a baby. I turned round in fear and there it was! The white cat! It was looking up at me and there was blood on its face! I looked at my hands. There was blood on them, too! I was still holding the piece of wood. "So you're still alive!" I screamed at the cat. I ran towards it and tried to hit it again. I banged the floor hard. I hit the cat over the head. I tried to hit it again, but it had disappeared. Then it appeared again in another corner of the room. It was looking at me with its red eyes. I ran after it and

tried to hit it. Every time I tried to do this, the cat disappeared. Every time it appeared it was red with blood. Soon its whole body was red with blood, but it appeared again and again. Here! There! In front of me! Behind me! On the floor! On the bed! In the air! At last the crying stopped. The cat disappeared and didn't come back.

All these things have happened in my mind, I thought. It was my imagination, just my imagination. I must control myself. Let me see. What was I doing? Yes. The plug. I was looking for the plug. I must find it. I'm a prisoner in my own room. The ghost is playing tricks on me. If I find the plug, I can send it away.

I got down on my knees to look for the plug. It was still on the floor beside my bed. I went towards it slowly and quietly like a cat. The plug was a bird and I was a cat. "I'm going to catch you, little bird," I whispered. Nearer and nearer. I held my breath and jumped! The plug was in my hands. I had it! I had it! It didn't move away from me. Now I must find the socket. I touched the wall with my fingers. The socket. Yes. Here it is. The ghost didn't pull the plug out of my hands. I put the plug into the socket and the light came on.

I got into bed and lay back. At last! My room was full of light. I looked round the room and couldn't believe my eyes. There wasn't any broken glass on the floor. The wardrobe wasn't on the floor. The window wasn't broken. All the things in my room were in order. The photo of Julie was on the wall. Julie's face was smiling down at me. The wardrobe was in its place in the corner of the room. The wardrobe door was shut. I got up and opened it. My clothes were in the wardrobe. Julie's dress was there too. My chair was in its place. I went to the bedroom door and tried to open it. It opened easily. I shut it again.

Then I began to laugh at myself. "I imagined all these things," I said. "The dance, the cat – it's just my imagination." I went back to bed. I looked at my bedside clock. It was 3.30. I sat in bed for about ten minutes. I was thinking. The light was on, but I could feel something strange. The ghost was still in the room. I had put the plug back, but the ghost was still there! It has broken the last rule of the game, I thought. I've put the plug in, but it hasn't gone away!

This thought filled me with panic and terror! The ghost had broken all the rules now: it didn't disappear when the light came on. I switched the light off (from the switch) but the 'evil presence' was still there. I pulled the plug out and put it back a number of times, but the ghost stayed in the room. The room was in order but full of evil.

I switched off the light and tried to sleep, but I couldn't. Then I tried to sleep with the light on, but I couldn't. In the end I turned the light off and lay in bed. The moon was still shining brightly. The ghost didn't play any tricks now; it stayed in my room quietly. It was 'there' all the time. I lay in bed and listened, but the room was silent. I could hear my heart. I could hear my own breathing.

I lay in bed for a long time. My eyes were open. I could see every detail of my room in the moonlight. Suddenly, I heard heavy breathing. It was coming from a corner of the room. Then I saw a dark shadow in the corner of the room. It was like a black cloud. The sound of heavy breathing was coming from the shadow. The shadow began to move towards me very slowly. I tried to jump out of bed but couldn't move in my fear. I lay there and the thin black cloud came nearer and nearer and nearer. Soon it was high in the air above my bed. I looked up at it. Then it began to come down on me. The room was now in complete darkness. The shadow cut out the moonlight. Soon it was over me and all round me. I could still hear heavy breathing. I could feel hot breath on my face: the breath of an evil ghost. I tried to scream, but couldn't. I couldn't breathe.

At the same time I could hear another sound. It came from outside. It was the sound of a cat outside my window. The cat was crying like a baby.

I lay under the dark shadow. I knew it was the shadow of death.

CHAPTER NINE

Today is Tuesday

Last night I was in the shadow of death, but I'm still alive. At the moment I'm in my study and I'm writing this story. It's only 10.00 p.m. but I'm very tired. You see, I didn't sleep a minute last night.

The shadow I have already described didn't harm me. When the morning light came, the shadow disappeared. I got up and left my bedroom. The shadow disappeared, but the ghost was still in the room. In fact, it's still there now.

I'm in my study now and the ghost can't harm me here (I hope!). I came to my study at 5.30 this morning. I've been writing this story since that time. My desk is full of papers. I've been writing for more than sixteen hours and I'm still writing. I haven't eaten. I haven't washed and I'm still wearing my pyjamas. It's cold outside. My pyjamas are made of thin material – but I can't feel the cold. I can only feel one thing: I'm very, very tired.

I'm near the end of my story. In one long day I've tried to describe my life since Julie's death. Perhaps you don't believe that any of these things happened. Perhaps you think I'm mad. Perhaps you are saying: You're a murderer and your conscience has punished you. Perhaps you think there was no ghost – only my conscience: my conscience invented the ghost. If you think any of these things you're wrong. All these things really happened.

My story began with a playful poltergeist and ended with an evil ghost. At the beginning we played a happy game.

But in time this game became a dangerous one. This game has continued for twelve years and Julie was my wife for twelve years. The game is like my life with Julie. At the beginning I was happy with her, but I became jealous of her friends. Then my mind became evil and I destroyed Julie and destroyed our life together. I wanted Julie to be mine and only mine. The same thing happened in the game. At the beginning it was a happy one. Then the ghost became jealous. It wanted me to be alone. It became evil and has tried to destroy me.

Now there's only one question on my mind: will the ghost destroy me?

At the moment, I'm trying not to think about this question. I'll find out the answer when I go to bed. I don't want to think about it now.

But what can I think about? The things I used to think about aren't important to me any more. Filbert Wiley's adventures are like a dream. The game with the ghost has become my whole life. But I know I can stop the game and change my life. There's one way I can do it. I must tell this secret to someone. Then I know the game will stop. Tomorrow Louis will be here, but I won't play chess with him. I'll tell him this story. Then I'll be all right again. What will Louis think when I tell him this story? I don't know. The game will end if I tell Louis the secret – but that's a big 'if'. Will I tell Louis my secret? I don't know. If I live through the night, then I'll certainly tell him. If I don't live, if I don't tell Louis my story – then it will be in this manuscript. Perhaps Louis will find this manuscript and publish it. But what a manuscript! There are papers all over my desk. There aren't any numbers on the pages. I've written it all in pencil and it's hard to read. There aren't any full stops or commas. If Louis wants to publish the manuscript, he'll have to edit it. I think he can edit it very well. I haven't thought of a good title for the book. Perhaps *Dangerous Game* is a good title. But my fears are running away with me. I'm not going to die. I'll edit the manuscript and publish the book myself. Louis will never see this manuscript.

It has been a strange day: strange in many ways. I haven't written a word for a month, but today I've written a whole book. It's January 22nd – twelve years to the day since Julie's death. We've been together for twenty-four years. What a day it has been! Yesterday the sun shone in a clear sky. But today it has been dark and cloudy – a real winter's day. I'll remember today for a long time.

During the day, while I've been writing, I've looked out of the window a few times. Now it's dark, of course. But earlier my garden was empty – no cats or anything like that. But I haven't had time to look out of the window very much. My story has been on my mind all day. I've tried to remember every detail. I've tried to tell you every detail.

Try to imagine me at this moment. I'm sitting at my desk. My desk light is on. I haven't drawn the curtains of my study. The moon is up and I can see it through my study window. I'm alone in this big house. The house is dark and silent. My bedroom is at the other end of the house and I know that sooner or later I must go to it. The bedroom door is shut, but I know someone is behind it. I know Julie's ghost is in the room. I know the ghost is waiting for me. I'll go into an evil world when I go into that room. When you're afraid, you look behind you all the time. You don't like the dark. Remember when you were a child? My bed used to be against the wall when I was a child. I never slept with my face towards the wall. I was afraid there was 'something' behind me. I still have this fear. Tonight I have to go into my bedroom alone, and perhaps I'll never come out of it again alive.

I've always been afraid of ghosts. When I was a child, I used to draw my curtains and then look at them. There were flowers on my curtain material, but I always used to see faces in those flowers. Sometimes they were happy faces, sometimes they were evil faces. When I turned off the light, I used to imagine these faces in the room all round me. Sometimes I used to cry and my mother used to come into the room. But if I cry tonight, who will come into my room? Who will say, "It's all right, darling. Go to sleep now. You've had a bad dream"? No one: I'll be alone. Alone with Poldy – Julie – the ghost.

You will ask: Why don't you leave the house? There's still time. Don't stay here. Don't play the game tonight. But I *must* play the game once more. I'm very sleepy, but I'll wake up when the game begins. I always wake up.

Why don't I phone Louis? He can come here and keep me company tonight. I'll tell you something. I've tried to phone Louis a number of times this evening, but my line is dead. I hear nothing when I pick up the phone. I'm cut off from the world.

So there's only one thing I can do: I must play the game. What kind of game will it be tonight? I tremble when I think about it. My heart is full of fear. My hand is shaking now while I'm writing these words. What will happen? I'll go into the bedroom. I won't have to pull out the plug to bring the ghost because the ghost is there already. I'll go to bed and the game will begin. But what kind of game will it be? How will it end?

I know I'm talking too much – writing too much. I haven't got any more to tell you, so why am I writing? Because I want you to keep me company. I'm writing because I'm afraid to leave this study. I'm all right here, but when I stop I'll have to go to my bedroom. I think that time has come now. I must stop now. So I'll say 'goodnight' to you – or perhaps it's 'goodbye'. Perhaps it's goodbye – forever.

CHAPTER TEN
Postscript

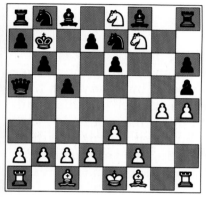

My name is Louis. I was William Harris's friend – as you already know from his story. I have added this postscript to his book to complete the story. William died on the night of January 22nd, 1976. A police doctor told me he died just before midnight: that is, about an hour after he went to bed.

Why did William die? No one can explain that. It's a mystery like so many things in his story. His life was a mystery and his death was a mystery too. William had no family and I was his only friend. The police have asked me many questions about William, but I haven't been able to tell them more than is in his book. Several police officers read William's manuscript. Some of them believe his story, others don't believe it. His death is a mystery.

I found the manuscript of *Dangerous Game* in William's study on the night after his death. Several days later, the police let me take the manuscript home. The whole manuscript was in the study just as William had left it. There were papers all over the desk and all over the floor. There were several pencils on the desk as well.

I'm writing this postscript six months after William's death. I've just finished my work on his manuscript. William wrote *Dangerous Game* (I think the title is a good one and I have kept it) in one long day. But I needed six months to edit his work. There weren't any numbers on the pages, so I needed a long time to put them in order. William wrote the book very quickly and the manuscript was very hard to read.

He didn't use full stops, commas or capital letters. He didn't write in complete sentences. So it was very hard for me to turn the manuscript into a proper book. I've divided the work into chapters, so I hope it has been easy to read. I've given each chapter a title, but I haven't added a word to William's story and I haven't cut out anything. It's just as he wrote it. I've published this story because I think William wanted me to publish it.

During the time I've been editing the work I've asked myself many questions about William. Some of the answers to my questions are in William's book, but many aren't.

For example, I knew William wasn't well – in his mind, I mean. There was always something on his mind and I could see this every time we met. He didn't eat well and he didn't sleep well. I could see this too. During the year before his death he became thinner and thinner. He wasn't interested in food, in his work, in the chess games we played. In fact he wasn't interested in life itself. He was certainly interested in something, but this 'something' was a mystery to me. He never told me about it. It was his secret. I wanted to call a doctor, but he never let me. During the year before his death our games of chess had become silly. William never *played* any more. He often stopped during a game and looked up at the ceiling. He was trying to hear something. Do you remember, I once asked him about 'Poldy' and he didn't want to tell me anything? In his book he says there was a knocking sound from the room above. Was there *really* a knocking sound? I don't know. I never heard anything myself.

Was William mad? Did all these things *really* happen, or did he imagine them? I don't know. William certainly had a wonderful imagination. Perhaps you have read his Filbert Wiley stories. If you *have* read them, then you will know a lot about William's imagination. In one of these stories (I can't remember the title) Filbert Wiley is a prisoner in a haunted house. Perhaps you remember the scene. I thought of it when I read this book. William was a real writer. In his story William often says he was an 'uninteresting fellow'. It's true he didn't have an interesting life. (And what does interesting really mean?) But he certainly had an interesting mind. You can see his mind at work in his detective stories. You can see it at work in this book.

Did William murder Julie? Another interesting question! It isn't possible to say. I certainly know he loved her deeply.

Perhaps William *was* jealous, but he never showed it. He described Julie very well in his story. She was a wonderful person. We all loved her. Of course, she was very different in character from William. She drew people round her. She was always laughing and singing. She was very good company. She did William a lot of good. She showed him the world. He enjoyed his life with Julie. After her death he became a different person. He cut himself off from the world. He threw himself into his work. In the end, I was his only friend. That's because I had known him in the old days – when we were students. I knew him before he met Julie. I knew him very well, but there's still a lot I don't know about him. Did he murder Julie? I find this hard to believe. But, then, perhaps he did murder her. One strange fact is certainly true: William died on the date Julie died: January 22nd, twelve years after her death. I can't explain it.

I knew William wasn't well and I often asked him to leave his house. I asked him to come and stay with me, but he didn't want to leave his own place. Once or twice I offered to stay with him, but he didn't want my company. So, after our chess games on a Wednesday, I always went home. We never talked very much during our games. I always went to his house because I know he enjoyed my company and I enjoyed his. In his story he says he tried to phone me on the night of his death. He says the line was dead – but that's a mystery too. You see, I used the phone to call the police after I found him. The phone was in order. Did William imagine it was out of order? Was it really out of order? If so, how did this happen?

So either William's story is true or it isn't. If it *is* true, then we must accept it. William was the victim of an evil, jealous ghost. (Whose ghost? I can't say.) Perhaps the story *isn't* true. Then we must believe that William imagined it all. This means that he was the victim of his own imagination. In the end he really became mad: he didn't live in our world any more. His imagination killed him. This can happen, of course, but we will never know the answer to the mystery.

The only thing I can do now is to describe in detail the night of Wednesday, January 23rd.

I arrived at William's house at my usual time: just before 8 o'clock. The house was completely dark and this surprised me. There was usually a light on somewhere. I knocked at the front door and waited. There was no reply. This surprised me too. William usually opened the door at once. Perhaps he has gone out, I thought — but no, that's not possible. He doesn't often go out and he's always at home on a Wednesday. He has *never* been out on a Wednesday.

I knocked at the door more loudly, but there was still no reply. I tried to open the front door, but I couldn't. So I went to the back door. I knocked at this too and waited. Again there was no reply. I tried to open this door too, but couldn't. I called out "William!" very loudly several times. There was no answer. I threw a few small stones lightly at the windows upstairs. No one came to any of the windows. This is very strange, I thought. I went round the house and looked at all the windows on the ground floor. They were shut. But in the end, I found a small window that was open. It was the kitchen window at the back of the house. I climbed through it (and it wasn't easy!) and turned on the kitchen light.

The kitchen was in order. William lived alone, but he was a very tidy person. The room was clean and tidy. I went straight to the living room. We always played chess in this room. I turned on the light. Again, the room was in order. The chess board was on the table. The chess pieces were in a wooden box beside the board. That's strange, I thought. William usually puts the pieces on the board before I arrive.

He is always ready for a game. When I noticed this, I began to worry. I began to call out William's name louder and louder. The name 'William' rang through the empty house, but there was no reply. I went out of the living room and stood at the foot of the stairs. I called up the stairs: "William!" No one answered me.

All at once, worry became fear – fear for William! What was the matter? I ran upstairs, three steps at a time and went straight to the study. Perhaps he's still working and hasn't heard me, I thought. I knocked at the study door and waited. There was no light under the door. No one answered so I went in. I switched on the light. The room was very untidy. There were papers on the desk and on the floor. I didn't look at the papers at the time. It wasn't my business. I write books myself and I wouldn't want other people to read my manuscripts! I didn't know then that these papers were the manuscript of the book I have just edited. I discovered this later – when the police came. The police first read William's manuscript and after several days they let me have it.

When I left William's study, I didn't go straight to his bedroom for a very simple reason. Don't forget, it was only just after eight o'clock. It was too early for anyone to be in bed. I went to every other room in the house. I was calling his name all the time. In the end, there was only one more room: the bedroom, and I went to it.

The bedroom door was shut. I knocked at the door gently and waited. I knocked again. Nothing. I opened the door very gently: the room was quite dark. It was very cold in the room, I remember – but other parts of the house were warm. I began to tremble in William's room. I don't know why, but I felt a strange fear. It was as if someone was in the room – as if someone was watching me. (Perhaps I only imagined this!) I touched the wall to find the light switch, but in my panic (my heart was beating rather wildly) I couldn't find it.

Then I kicked something. I touched it: it was William's bedside table. I touched the top of the table and found the bedside lamp. I pressed the switch but the light didn't come on. Then I kicked something on the floor: it was the plug. I got down on my knees and found it. Why isn't it in the socket? I thought.

I put the plug into the socket and the light came on. When I stood up, I looked round the room. I couldn't believe my eyes! It was very untidy and in great disorder. Two windows were broken and there was glass on the floor. There were clothes on the floor, too – William's clothes and one of Julie's party dresses. The wardrobe was completely broken and there were pieces of wood on the floor. There were small pieces of paper, too. I picked up one or two pieces and realized they were part of a photograph. A cold wind blew through the broken windows. I could hear a cat out in the cold. It was crying like a baby, poor thing!

I wanted to run out of the room, but I had to find William first. The double bed was against the wall. There was a figure under the blankets. There was a pillow at the top end of the bed. It was over the head of the figure in the bed. I picked the pillow up very gently. It was right over William's face. I knew at once he was dead. The face filled me with horror. The eyes were wide open and the mouth was wide open, too. There were signs of fear and terror in William's face: signs of panic. The eyes stared up at me: they stared in horror.

I put the pillow back over William's face very gently. I didn't want to disturb anything before the police came. I stood in front of the body for a long time. I was too shocked to move. The whole room was evil, so evil!

While I stood there, I noticed something strange on the pillow. There was a clear imprint on it – like the imprint of a hand. It was as if a hand had pressed the pillow hard against William's face – as if a hand had held the pillow over William's face until he died.

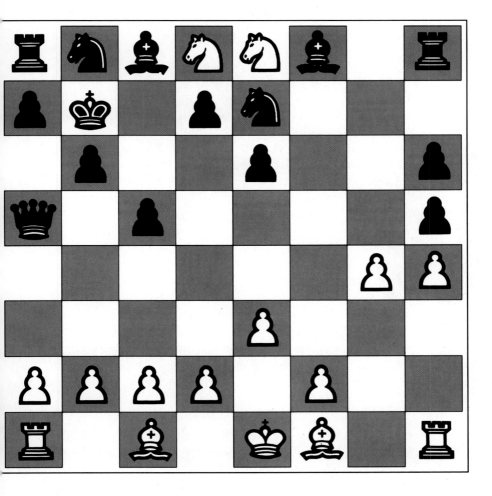

READING ACTIVITIES

Before reading

1 Here are some categories of stories – adventure, romance, mystery, science fiction, ghost, detective, spy, war, travel, historical, western. From its title, what sort of story do you think *Dangerous Game* might be?

2 "Some time after my wife died, I realized that my bedroom was haunted." The writer of *Dangerous Game* believes in ghosts. Do you? Why/why not? Ask another person their opinion.

While reading

1 Write out the summary below, putting *one* word only in each space. The information is in Chapter 2.

Poldy never ..... when I turned off the light with the ..... . He came only when I pulled the ..... out of its ..... . Poldy and I invented a ..... . This ..... had very simple ..... . When I put the plug back and the ..... came on, Poldy ..... . If Poldy ..... my ..... before I put the ..... back in, he ..... the game.

2 Rewrite the following with the correct information. The answers are in Chapters 1–5.

William and Julie were married for ten years before Julie became ill. After her death, William's friend, Louis, continued to visit him every Thursday night to play cards.

Meanwhile William played a secret game every night with Poldy, a character in one of William's detective stories. The games with Poldy quickly got dangerous. William's bedroom became a very happy place.

3 Read William's conversation with Louis in Chapter 3 and answer these questions:

a) "You haven't been watching the game, William." What game is Louis referring to?

b) "But you must be careful. Imagination can be dangerous." How can it be dangerous?

c) "But he's only a character in one of your stories." Who is Louis talking about?

4 When Louis goes home after the game of chess in Chapter 3, he is still worried about William. Imagine he tells his wife about William's strange behaviour that evening and write a short dialogue.

5 Put the following sentences in the correct sequence of events. The information is in Chapters 6–8.

William realised Poldy and Julie were really the same person. ☐

A great wind blew through the room. ☐

William held a pillow over Julie's photograph. ☐

A thin black cloud came over William's head. ☐

Julie's dress and photo began to dance beautifully. ☐

Something tore the photo into tiny pieces. ☐

William tried to kill the white cat. ☐

After reading

1 After Louis finds William's body in Chapter 10 he phones the police to report his friend's death. Imagine his conversation with the police officer on duty and write a short dialogue.

2 "Was William mad? Did all these things *really* happen, or did he imagine them?"

Louis asks himself this question after reading William's manuscript. What do you think? Discuss with a friend.

3 You are a newspaper reporter sent by your editor the day after William's death to cover the story. Call your story *Writer Dies in Mysterious Circumstances* and write a short account. Describe what sort of a life William led, who Louis was and how he found the body. Refer also to Julie's death twelve years before.

4 Complete the following puzzle:

```
 1                    □  — — —
 2   — — — —          □  — —
 3       — —          □  — — —
 4     — — —          □  —
 5       — —          □  — — —
 6       — —          □  — — — — —
 7     — — —          □  — — — — —
 8     — — —          □  — — — — —
 9       — —          □  —
10     — — —          □  — — —
11        —           □  — — —
```

Clues for the words across:

1 Poldy appears when this is pulled out.
2 How William felt towards Julie's friends.
3 William killed Julie with this.
4 It hangs on the bedroom wall.
5 The number of years William and Julie were married.
6 Julie's party dress is kept here.
7 The game with Poldy becomes this.
8 Filbert Wiley's profession.
9 How William's bedroom felt to Louis.
10 William's worst day of the week.
11 Where Louis finds the manuscript.

Clue for the word down:

It plays a dangerous game with William.

Material devised by Anne Collins and Jean Greenwood